THIS BOOK BELONGS TO

PUFFIN BOOKS

UK | USA | Canada | Ireland | Australia
India | New Zealand | South Africa | China

Penguin Books is part of the Penguin Random House group of companies
whose addresses can be found at global.penguinrandomhouse.com.

Penguin
Random House
Australia

First published by Penguin Group (Australia), 2015

Cover and internal design by Evi O. © Penguin Group (Australia)
Illustrations by Lucia Masciullo
Cover portrait © Tim de Neefe
Typeset in Bembo by Post Pre-press Group, Brisbane, Queensland
Colour separation by Splitting Image Colour Studio, Clayton, Victoria
Printed and bound in Australia by Griffin Press, an accredited ISO AS/NZS 14001
Environmental Management Systems printer.

National Library of Australia Cataloguing-in-Publication data available.

ISBN 978 0 14 330849 2

Photograph on p124 courtesy of Phil Eggman.

puffin.com.au
ouraustraliangirl.com.au

Charms on the front cover reproduced with kind permission from A&E Metal Merchants.
www.aemetal.com.au

OUR
AUSTRALIAN
GIRL

Meet Marly

It's 1983 and Marly is just trying to fit in at Sunshine Primary School. But being a refugee from Vietnam doesn't make things easy, and when Marly's cousins come to stay and end up at the same school, her friends make fun of them. How can Marly stay loyal to her cousins and keep her school friends as well?

Meet Marly and join in her adventure in the first of four exciting stories about a daring girl torn between two worlds.

Puffin Books

For Lina, Tina and Jessica

OUR
AUSTRALIAN
GIRL

Meet
Marly

Alice Pung

With illustrations by Lucia Masciullo

Puffin Books

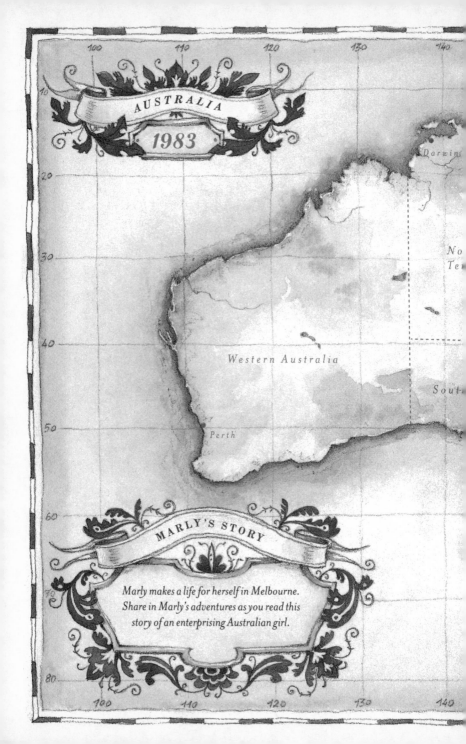

Where this story takes place

Lost and Found

MARLY was on her hands and knees on the kitchen floor, pretending to play Twister on a shower curtain patterned all over with big red and orange dots.

'Get off, Marlin!' shouted her father, who was also crouched on the floor, trying to stick together the three plastic shower curtains with duct tape. Marly had got to pick the designs on the curtains when they went to K-Mart yesterday. She'd wanted to choose the see-through ones with tumbling coloured umbrellas, but her dad said that the curtains had to be dark. So she'd chosen navy ones printed with massive coloured dots. The silver duct tape made the curtains look like an enormous calculator – or even an Atari computer game, thought Marly.

'Beep beep,' she giggled as she pressed the buttons.

'Stop mucking around and help me hold one end of this,' said Marly's dad.

They carried the three stuck-together shower curtains into the living room. There was a double bed at one end of the room, which her father had bought earlier that week from the St Vincent De Paul store.

Marly started to bounce up and down on it until her mother slapped her lightly over the ankles with a cloth measuring tape. 'Ay, get off there,' she scolded, 'or they'll arrive to a saggy bed. The kids will sink to the middle of it and disappear.' Her mother winked at her.

'Don't say such things!' said Marly's dad.

'You will bring them bad luck! They're not even here yet and already you are talking about disappearances. Aiyoh, this is very bad.'

Marly's Uncle Beng had been lost for more than seven years, but a year ago they had received a letter from him. He'd written that not only was he alive, but he had a wife and two children. They lived in a place called Hong Kong, and they wanted to come and live with Marly's family in Australia. Now it was only one week until they arrived.

Marly watched as her dad strung up a piece of rope from one end of the living room to the other, dividing the room down the middle. Then he hung up the taped shower curtains so that they made a wall separating the bed from the living area.

'When your uncle's family arrive,' he told Marly, 'you are not to go past this wall. Understand?'

'It's not a very good wall, Dad,' Marly said.

'If you bounce high enough on the sofa, you can see right over it.' She showed him.

He shook his finger at her. 'This space behind the curtain belongs to your uncle and his family. You have to respect their privacy.'

Marly looked over at the small bed island that was going to be her uncle's new home. Her two new cousins, Tuyet and DaWei, would be here this time next week, living behind that curtain. She knew nothing about them except that Tuyet was a twelve-year-old girl and DaWei was a seven-year-old boy.

'Those poor little kids,' her mother sighed, 'living in that refugee camp most of their lives, locked up behind a wire fence.'

Marly was quite worried. She knew that only bad people were locked up. She imagined her cousins in white pyjama-like outfits patterned with arrows, like the ones she'd seen in a book about Australian convicts. She wondered if she would have to hide her toys from them. Also, she felt a little resentful that her cousins were getting the best part of the living room where the window was. Marly had always wanted her own room, but this would never happen now. Their house would be getting smaller.

2
The Long-lost Cousins

'Your cousins will arrive with not very much,' Marly's mother explained to her that evening when they were snuggled up in their double bed. 'Just as we did. So you'll have to be a good cousin to them. You have to try and share.'

'No!' Marly cried. 'They'll wreck my things! You told me to let Beanshoot Baby hold my connector pen and he dribbled on it, and now the pink, green and yellow don't work!'

Beanshoot Baby was the baby that Marly

sometimes had to look after while the mothers worked on their sewing in the back shed.

Marly's mum sewed clothes for a living with two other women. Every two weeks, a man in a white van would deliver stacks of fabric pieces shaped like sleeves, shirt backs, skirt triangles and pant legs to each of their homes. Each woman would sew as much as she could of her pile, and then they would all meet up together at Marly's house to help each other do the finishing touches – putting spare buttons in little plastic bags to be stapled to the shirts, or opening buttonholes with a special tool. Often the other women would bring their children who were too small for school, and if it happened to be during Marly's school holidays, Marly would have to look after them while the mothers worked.

'Beanshoot Baby is smaller than you,' said Marly's mum, 'so you've got to be the bigger girl if he breaks things. You don't have to share everything, but your cousins don't have very much. Maybe you could pick out a few toys that you wouldn't mind them having. That way, you can save all your good toys and keep them hidden in our room.'

Marly still did not like the sound of this. Most of the time, she didn't think too much about how different she was from her friends at school, but things like this made Marly aware that her family was very different. Kylie and Jessica *never* had to give away their toys. Sure, they would lend them to Marly to play with, but they'd never let Marly *have* their stuff. Marly hated how unfair her parents were being. Her stuff should be hers to keep, she thought.

'Ma, why were they locked up?' Marly asked. 'What did they do wrong?' She hoped that this would remind her mother that her cousins were not to be trusted and would probably wreck her things.

'Marly!' Her mother looked shocked and then sad. 'They didn't do anything wrong. Back in Vietnam, where we all lived once, the country was divided into two sides – the North and the South. There was a war, and when the war ended the North won, but the South was still richer than the North. So the government from the North decided to take things away from the people of the South.'

'Oh, you mean like Robin Hood, stealing from the rich to give to the poor?' Marly asked. 'That's not such a bad thing.'

'Your uncle was from a rich family.'

'Oh.'

'He had his own printing business. He worked very hard to make it successful. They took it away from him and locked him up for years. When he finally got out last year, he had no money, no house, no business. He found his family and ran away to Hong Kong with them. Then they all got locked up because the Hong Kong government didn't want any more refugees in their country.'

'What's a refugee?' asked Marly.

'People like us. People like your uncle and his family. People who have had to leave their homes and come to a new place.'

Marly wasn't so sure she counted as a refugee. She had been here since she was two, and she could barely remember anything about her life back in Vietnam or the boat journey to Australia. Marly once had a friend at school, Hai, who hadn't spoken much English when he'd come to Sunshine Primary School. She'd had to explain everything to him in Cantonese: how you couldn't just walk home during lunchtime, how boys and girls toilets were separate, and how you couldn't wear flannelette pyjamas to school. He hadn't even known what 'play equipment' was, so Marly had had to show him how to go down the slide.

After a week, though, they were both hurtling down the slide head-first, balancing across the high wooden beams behind the school timber benches, and racing each other around the yard.

Marly had never been happier at lunchtime, though class time was a different matter. Other kids called Hai a 'chink' when the teacher couldn't hear. They told Marly after school that he was 'fresh off the boat', and that girls shouldn't be hanging around with boys. But Marly didn't care – he had become her best friend, and they shared a secret language. Two years later, Hai's family moved house and Marly never saw him again. She'd spent months sitting by herself at lunch, until Jessica and Kylie came along. Even though Marly wasn't sure she even liked hanging out with them, it sure beat being alone.

Marly didn't know what cousin Tuyet would be like, but cousin DaWei would be the same age as Hai was when she met him. The thought made her feel happy. The next morning, Marly generously picked out an assortment of things she no longer played with – her old Rubik's cube with all the stickers peeled off and stuck back on so that each side matched but looked a bit ragged, her Sindy doll, some bouncy balls she'd got from a twenty-cent vending machine, an old truck her father's friend had given her thinking she was a boy because of her haircut, and her broken Duracell bunny.

She would be the bigger girl, just like her mother wanted her to be.

3
The Arrival

It was Marly's first time at an airport. There were lots of loud people holding signs and waving madly at their families. Marly watched an old man emerge from a lift in a wheelchair that was pushed by a lady in a blue uniform. She saw bunches of flowers bigger than a person's head and stuffed koalas in cork hats holding little Australian flags.

Marly's family had brought along no such gifts or surprises, but when her dad first spotted his brother and family, he yelled and waved them over, not caring who turned their heads to see what all the commotion was about.

'Ay, Beng!' hollered Marly's dad. 'Beng!
Aiyoh, Beng, you old fatso! We're over here!'

'Duong! Wah, look at you, you toothpick!'
yelled Marly's new uncle when he spotted
them.

Her uncle was the opposite of fat, Marly
thought. In fact, his white shirt and blue
trousers were too big for him. It seemed that
the only thing keeping him from disappearing
into his clothes was the big brown leather belt
he wore around his waist. Marly's father, on
the other hand, had developed a little bit of
a belly. She wondered why they were calling
each other these bizarre names.

As her uncle and dad whacked each other
on the shoulders, Marly suddenly noticed
her aunty standing behind them, looking
embarrassed. 'Stop behaving like peasants!'
she heard her whisper. Aunty Tam was slender
and wore a pleated sleeveless dress. Her hair

surrounded her face like wispy black feathers, and she had very large brown eyes. She was so elegant! And so young! Marly had expected someone more like her mother, who had a Maggi-noodle perm and was wearing a blue Adidas tracksuit.

She gazed at her cousins.

Cousin Tuyet's long black hair was parted down the middle like a set of curtains framing blinking bewildered eyes and a massive mouth. She wore a pair of purple pants and a knitted jumper with a snowflake on the front. She even had a scarf around her neck with pom-poms hanging from the end of it. Marly noticed that her cousin's fingernails and toenails were painted hot pink. She had little gold rings in her ears.

'Say hello to your new cousin,' Aunty Tam commanded.

'Allo!' grinned Tuyet, giving a little wave of her hand.

Marly was too surprised to wave back. How grown-up Tuyet looked. In fact, she didn't even look poor at all. Instantly, Marly did not like her new cousin. She got the feeling that Tuyet was probably one of those girls who liked hanging around adults and acted snooty towards younger kids. One of those girls who tried too hard.

Marly's mother nudged her from behind. 'Say hello to your cousin Tuyet.'

'Aren't you hot?' asked Marly.

'Wah, she sounds just like an Australian!' laughed Uncle Beng. 'Direct and to the point.'

'Marly!' scolded her mother, but it was a fake scold, because Marly knew she had said what her mother was thinking.

Aunty Tam said, 'Oh dear. Oh my. We thought Australia would be cold, because it's beneath Hong Kong. Is it very warm outside?'

'Are you kidding me?' exclaimed Marly's dad. 'Hah! It's thirty-two degrees!'

Her other cousin, DaWei, was very small, shorter than Marly by at least half a head. He hid behind his mother, peering from behind her with the same large puppy-like eyes as Tuyet. He wore a tan tracksuit with an enormous dog's face on the front, and green running shoes.

'Come meet your new cousin MyLinh,' coaxed Aunty Tam. 'Come on, don't be shy.' It had been ages since anyone had called Marly by her Chinese name. She hoped that it would not become a habit.

DaWei came out from behind his mother and looked at Marly.

'We flew here on a plane,' said DaWei. 'Have you ever been on a plane?'

'No.'

'Of course she hasn't, silly,' his sister told him. 'They came here on a boat before us.'

Marly's dad had to take the kids home first and then come back for Uncle Beng and Aunty Tam, because there was not enough room in the Datsun for all of them. Marly's mum stayed behind to keep their new relatives company as Marly and her new cousins climbed into the car.

4
Homecoming

MARLY'S cousins stared out the car window at their new country.

'The cars here go so fast!' exclaimed DaWei.

'It's the freeway,' Marly told them. 'We're going to Sunshine.' She was starting to feel good about her new role. This was how she had felt when explaining things for the first time to her friend Hai. She'd watch as he stared at her with his mouth wide open and then burst out laughing. 'You're joking, right? People sit on toilet seats instead of squatting on them? Come on, Marly, don't lie!' he'd laugh. She missed him.

'Sunshine?' asked Tuyet in English. 'Like, on a warm day?'

'That's the name of our suburb.'

Instead of being grateful that Marly was being so helpful, Cousin Tuyet simply asked another question: 'What's a suburb?'

Before Marly had a chance to explain, the car was passing Highpoint Shopping Centre. 'Look at that!' exclaimed DaWei. 'It's enormous!'

'It's a shopping centre,' explained Marly. 'You can buy anything you want from there.'

'Wah!' exclaimed DaWei. 'Can we go here one day, Uncle? Can we?'

'Of course, my boy.'

Marly thought it was very rude to ask adults for things, and she could just imagine her dad taking DaWei to Highpoint – he would be the type of kid to point at things and tug on her father's sleeve until he drove him crazy.

Soon they were in Marly's neighbourhood with its concrete houses in white and pastel colours and loud dogs behind steel mesh fences with peeling paint on the posts.

'Are you rich, Uncle?' asked DaWei.

Marly thought it was another very rude question to ask, but Marly's father only laughed loudly, as if it were the funniest thing he'd ever heard. 'No, son. Whatever gave you that idea?'

'Some of these houses have two or three cars parked out the front!'

'Hah! They probably don't work,' explained Marly's father. 'Look over there – that house has at least four rusting car engines on the lawn.'

'But the houses are so big!'

'Compared to Hong Kong they are,' agreed Marly's dad.

'Well, here we are.' He parked the car and unlocked the house. Her cousins stood at the doorway, hesitating, wide-eyed, until her father guided them through and carried their bags inside.

'You kids must be tired,' he said. 'Marly, why don't you give your cousins a snack. Show them around.'

Marly felt proud that she was given this responsibility. She felt as if she was trusted with showing her cousins a new world. But first she had to feed them. She went into the kitchen and her cousins followed.

'Wah, sister, it's massive!' exclaimed DaWei.

Marly went to the cupboard and brought out the box of Coco Pops. She filled two bowls and then, to be fancy and keep up the impression that they were very sophisticated, brought out two glasses and filled them with milk. 'Sit down and eat,' she said. She was going to show them how to pour the milk into the cereal, a little bit at a time so the rice puffs would not get soggy, but DaWei and Tuyet had already dug in.

'Mmm,' DaWei said, 'tiny chocolate cookies.' They were eating their Coco Pops dry from the bowl, only stopping occasionally to take a sip of milk from the glass. Marly decided not to tell them they were meant to put milk in. She kind of liked dry Coco Pops too.

When they had finished, Marly showed them their side of the living room. 'This is where you will sleep,' she said, guessing that they would be as pleased as she was with the arrangement.

DaWei loved the shower-curtain wall that revealed the double bed and small single bed wedged at the bottom end of it. He jumped from one to the other. He also loved looking out the window.

'This place is massive!' he cried.

Marly grinned.

'Wah,' said Tuyet. 'Feel this bed. It's very

soft.' She sat on the edge of the mattress and patted it in awe, as if she were sitting on a cloud. 'It looks like a bed you would see on television.'

Marly had never been one of those kids at school who had the latest clothes or games, but today she felt seriously rich. There were so many things she had that her cousins wanted and loved. She wasn't used to it. 'Come on, it's just a boring bed. You're acting like you've never seen a bed before,' Marly said.

Tuyet just looked at her, and suddenly Marly realised that perhaps this was the first bed her cousin had ever sat on. She pointed towards DaWei's Cathay Pacific bag. 'What do you have in there?' she asked.

'We got these bags on the plane,' explained DaWei. 'Books and toys and things. Do you want to see?'

Suddenly, Marly found Tuyet's Cathay Pacific backpack on her lap. 'You can keep three things out of there,' said Tuyet.

'Ooh! Thanks!' Marly could not believe her luck. She carefully tipped out the contents of the backpack on the floor and began to pore over the small cardboard box of pencils, the colouring book, the plush plane and the stencils.

Then she remembered her manners and what her mother had asked her to do.

'Wait! I'll be back,' she said. She ran into the bedroom she shared with her parents and pulled out the box of toys she had saved. Bringing it to her cousin's side of the living room, she said generously, 'You can have a look in here and see if there is anything you would like to have.'

DaWei dived right in, and claimed the Duracell bunny. 'Hey look, sister, look at this!' The bunny had a drum strapped to its furry chest, and in each paw was a wooden drumstick. With operating batteries in its back, it would beat the drum; but the battery cover was missing, and one of the drumsticks was broken off at the middle.

Tuyet picked up the Rubik's cube. 'I had one of these . . .' she said, and twisted it around.

'Stop!' cried Marly. 'It took me ages to peel all of the stickers off and stick them back so the colours match on each side. You can't mess it up – you'll never be able to put it together again!'

Marly had given these toys to her cousins and they were no longer hers, so she knew she shouldn't have been so bossy about what they would do with them; but it was hard to see someone else mess up your old toys. Tuyet ignored Marly, and twisted the cube this way and that, until the shapes were completely jumbled.

I bet she did that on purpose, thought Marly. Stupid cousin – I bet she thinks she's too good to have my old toys. She will destroy everything!

The truth was, Marly had not expected Tuyet to be so tall, or so cool and grown-up, with her painted nails and beautiful mum. She thought that her poor locked-up cousins would both look more like DaWei, skinny and wide-eyed adorable, his face filling with joy over her old stuffed toys.

But as Marly watched closely, she could see that Tuyet's hands were doing something hers had never been able to do. The colours were starting to line up on each side again: the blues with the blues, the yellows with the yellows. Soon, Marly could see that her cousin was going to achieve the impossible – she was going to solve the Rubik's puzzle! And sure enough, in less than ten minutes, Tuyet had all the coloured sides matching again. She handed the cube back to Marly. 'It's pretty easy,' she said with a modest shrug.

Marly knew it would be pointless asking her cousin to show her how she did it, because the cube would be jumbled differently each time. Instead, she said, 'It's yours now.' But she felt an unfamiliar jealousy surge in the middle of her chest. Surely, she was supposed to be the one showing things to her new cousins, not the other way around.

5

An Extended Family

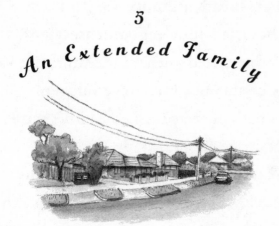

WHEN the adults arrived home, Marly's aunty and uncle exclaimed over the house. 'Look how high the ceilings are!' 'Incredible, the walls are so cool and sturdy.' 'Look at the beautiful wallpaper!' Marly thought that the brown and green paisley print was horrible, but maybe Uncle Beng had no taste after being locked up for so long.

'Aw, come on, brother, it's nothing special. This is one of the poorer properties in this country.'

'Then this must be a very lucky country

indeed,' breathed Aunty Tam.

They had four big suitcases with them. After she started unpacking, Aunty Tam asked if she could put a box in the kitchen.

'What's in there?' asked Marly's mum.

'Our rice cooker.'

'You brought a rice cooker to Australia?' laughed Marly's mum. 'But we already have a rice cooker. And a microwave too!'

'But this rice cooker is a National branded one, the best. We've had it since the refugee camp. We cooked all our meals in it. By the way, sister, what's a microwave?'

Marly's mum took Aunty Tam by the elbow and led her into the kitchen to show her.

Over the next few weeks her uncle's family settled in. Mealtimes were much livelier now that there were seven people around the table instead of three. Marly's father liked to tell terrible Dad jokes. Other times, the adults would talk, forgetting that the kids were still listening at the table. 'I'm not sure what happened to Old Aunt Pek,' said Uncle Beng gravely. 'When I last saw her, she knew they were taking me away for re-education, and she gave me the gold Buddha around her neck. She said it would protect me from harm.'

'She's probably gone,' sighed Marly's mother.

'Let me tell you, Duong, they worked us like slaves at that re-education camp! It was like a prison. And they took away my Buddha. They said it was a sign of greed because he was made of gold and so fat!'

'Hah!' laughed the adults, though Marly didn't understand what was so funny.

Although Tuyet liked to spend most of her time indoors, DaWei and Marly were always outside. They went on wild adventures around the house, looking for secret trapdoors. They pretended to be soldiers going to war, wearing pots over their heads as helmets and carrying rulers as swords. When no adults were looking, they even climbed the huge plum tree in the front yard and tried to leap off it onto the verandah.

DaWei taught Marly how to fold water bombs out of the Bi-Lo ads that came in the mail every Tuesday, and they had water fights on hot days. Marly had thought she would be too old to hang around with her little cousin, but she actually liked playing with him more than with Tuyet.

Tuyet had her talents too, though: she knew how to make amazing toys with things that Marly had thought of as junk. She folded origami animals from food wrappers, and made painted shields for Marly and DaWei out of Danish biscuit tin lids and foil. She also narrated stories for DaWei and Marly to act out, and they were always better than anything Marly could have made up herself. She and her cousins ate Coco Pops for breakfast and sometimes lunch, and often as a snack.

6
Jackie and Jermaine

ONE evening, Marly's father came home from his job at the Felix Food Factory with an enormous box.

'Oh no, Duong,' sighed Marly's mum. 'You brought home peanut butter again.'

Marly's father got cheap discounts on jams, peanut butter and other things Marly's mum didn't know how to use, like custard powder and cheese sauce mix. Marly wished that the factory made Nutella.

'No, this is even better!' proclaimed Marly's Dad. 'It's a television! I bought it after work from Spiros. He had it in his car boot. It's his old one, but it's still in colour. He even included the antenna.'

Marly and her cousins crowded around the television and helped him set it up. Marly was so excited! Now she would be able to talk about the shows the other kids talked about at recess at school, instead of just pretending she knew about them: the Sooty Show, the Muppets, Danger Mouse.

Television didn't change their evening lives too much, because the adults hogged it, watching boring adult shows and the seven o'clock news. Marly wondered why the only Asians on TV seemed to be moustached kung fu masters, villains or criminals. During the day, while it was still school holidays, Marly and DaWei spent entire mornings and afternoons in front of the television, watching the children's shows on Channel 2.

'You lazy kids,' Aunty Tam scoffed. 'Why

can't you be helpful like Tuyet?'

It was true – Tuyet rarely watched the television. Instead, she was always helping her mum and Marly's mum wash dishes, sweep the floors, peel vegetables or snip loose threads from the clothes they made.

'Marly, DaWei, come and help us shell peas!' called her mother.

What an annoying suck-up Tuyet is, thought Marly. She ruins it for all of us. Marly picked up a small rubber ball and hurled it at the television to turn it off. Instead, she knocked some incense out of their family urn on the mantelpiece.

'Aiyoh!' cried her mother when she entered the room to see what the noise was about. 'You can't keep still for one moment, can you? You always have to go and destroy things!' Marly's mum scooped the incense back into the urn with her hands. 'You're just lucky you didn't topple it over.' The urn was in front of a photograph of Marly's grandparents, who had died during the Vietnam war. Every week, Marly's mum would light incense in front of the urn to honour the memory of her own parents.

Marly glared at Tuyet – it was her fault Marly was always in trouble.

The summer holidays were nearly over. Tuyet and DaWei had been enrolled at Marly's school, and two weeks before school started, Marly heard Tuyet drilling her little brother behind their curtain on a Saturday morning.

'Spell ball,' Tuyet told DaWei.

'B-A-L-L,' replied DaWei, scratching his head.

'Spell bat.'

'B-A-T.'

'Spell bicycle.'

'B-I-C-Y-C-L-E.'

'Spell beautiful.'

'B-E-U . . .'

'No!' corrected Tuyet. 'B-E-A-U-T-I-F-U-L! Now let's do some sums. Seven times eight.'

'Fifty-six,' DaWei replied almost immediately, still scratching his head.

'Nine times eight.'

'Seventy-two.'

Marly could not believe it. She couldn't spell those last two words when she was in Grade One. She found it incredible that these two cousins, who had only spoken to her in Cantonese, could spell words perfectly in English. And they knew up to at least their nine-times tables! They were geniuses! She wondered what else they were hiding from her.

'Hey kids, you guys are really good at maths,' said Marly's father, overhearing them. He was sitting on the couch, reading the local paper. Uncle Beng was next to him filling in some forms. 'Marlin here is very bad at it. Aren't you, my girl? I always tell her: Marly, without geometry, life is pointless. Ha! Ha! Pointless!'

Marly hated how her father laughed at his own jokes, which no one got except for him.

'But she is good at other things, eh?' He ruffled Marly's hair. 'Like talking in English. I swear, this girl went to school and about three months later she was speaking like a local. Speaking non-stop, too!'

'Stop it, Dad!'

'Hee hee. Marly, what English names should we give your cousins for school?' Marly's father asked her.

'What's wrong with the names they already have?' asked Uncle Beng. 'Tuyet means "snow", and DaWei was a special name given to us by a Hong Kong friend, who told us it meant "big and great" in Mandarin.'

Big and Great, thought Marly. Oh boy.

The kids at school are really going to love a boy who calls himself Big and Great. And there was no snow ever, not in Melbourne anyway.

'I like Fanny,' piped Tuyet. 'There was a girl at the camp named Fanny Yip.'

'No, that's a terrible name!' said Marly. 'Kids will laugh at you.'

'Why? I like fans.'

'Yes, tell us, Marlin,' Marly's dad asked, turning towards her, 'why is that a bad name?'

Marly didn't answer. Instead, she said, 'Why don't you call yourself Jackie?'

'That's a boy's name!'

'No, it's not. If you call yourself Jackie then your brother can call himself Jermaine and we would all match, like the Jackson 5!'

When Marly's family had arrived in Australia, the first song they'd heard over the radio was 'I Want You Back' by a band called the Jackson 5. It was one of the strangest, most beautiful and exciting songs Marly had ever heard. The only part of it she understood was when the lead singer went through the first three letters of the alphabet – A–B–C. The Jackson 5 were always on the radio then. Before they came on, the announcer would always say, 'Before there was "Off the Wall" or "Thriller", before Michael went solo, there were the Jackson 5: Michael, Marlon, Tito, Jermaine, Jackie and Randy!'

Her father had suggested Marlin as a good Australian name for her because he thought that was what the girl in the Jackson 5 was called, and it also sounded a lot like her real name, MyLinh. Marly loved it. It was only much later that she'd found out all the Jackson 5 were boys. Even worse, the name Marlin was actually spelt 'Marlon'!

Luckily, when she'd started school, none of the kids had realised she had a boy's name. And Marly had never told anyone about the mistake. Anyway, there was already a boy in her class called Jesse, who had the sides of his head shaved, and another boy who smelled like Imperial Leather soap called Kim, and a popular girl who called herself Sammy. So Marly thought that Jackie and Jermaine were excellent names.

'No way!' Tuyet was horrified.

'It's better than Fanny.'

Uncle Beng looked quite pleased. 'Jackie, ay?' he muttered. 'Jackie, Jackie, I like it. But it does sound like a boy's name. So DaWei, you can be called Jackie, and Tuyet, you can be called Jermaine.'

'Jackie's good,' smiled DaWei. 'Like Jackie Chan.'

'Who's that?' asked Marly.

'A famous Hong Kong actor.'

'We've never heard of him.' She hated how her cousins were always name-dropping famous people they'd heard of in Hong

Kong, as if they were hanging out with stars all the time.

'Yeah, well, you will soon.'

Marly stuck out her tongue.

'But I don't like Jermaine,' protested Tuyet. 'It's not a pretty name. What about Cinderella?'

'Oh nooooo.' Marly put her palms on either side of her face and made her mouth into a massive 'O'. 'The kids at school will really, really tease you.'

'You make this school out to be so bad,' complained Tuyet, 'as if it's filled with kids who will pick on you for any small thing. I bet the kids won't even care when they find out that DaWei and I know our times tables up to fourteen times fourteen.'

Show-off, thought Marly sourly.

'The kids will tease you at school for being know-it-alls,' she said. And worst of all, she would be related to them.

'What kind of ridiculousness is this?' scoffed Aunty Tam as she came in, dressed in a sequinned pink shirt and pleated white skirt that fell past her knees. She had a string of pearls around her neck, and black high heels on. 'Marly, stop making up such madness to scare your cousins. No one picks on kids for being smart. They respect them. Now, who wants to go to the supermarket with me?'

'Me! Me!' cried Tuyet and DaWei.

'I think our kids have head lice,' said Aunty Tam, and suddenly they didn't look so eager.

That night, Marly watched as Uncle Beng filled out the school forms with DaWei and Tuyet's new English names. He wrote down: *Jackie* and *Germainn*. Marly was still so cross with Tuyet that she didn't tell her uncle that he'd spelt Jermaine wrong.

7

Marly's Bowl Haircut

'TIME for haircuts!' called Uncle Beng from the backyard. He was sitting in his shorts and singlet. It was so hot Marly thought you could probably break an egg on the cement ground and it would begin to fry. Except, of course, an egg was food, and her family never wasted food.

'Me first!' DaWei came bounding outside and sat on the little stool in front of his dad.

That afternoon, Aunty Tam had returned from the chemist with a big bottle of something that smelled suspiciously like pee. She lathered it all over DaWei's and Tuyet's hair, and then made Marly do it as well, and then the adults put it in each other's hair. Marly's mum and aunty had also washed out all the sheets and blankets and hung them to dry in the sun.

Uncle Beng put a big plastic soup bowl over DaWei's head, like a helmet. DaWei looked like the Hot Soup Superhero, sitting there smiling and tapping his feet on the concrete. Uncle Beng started to cut around the helmet, being careful around the ears. When he was done, he lifted the bowl from DaWei's head. 'Ta-dah!' he exclaimed.

DaWei's black hair was perfectly bowl-shaped. He looked like a mushroom, or one of those olden-day monks that Marly had seen in a history book once. The ones who wore brown sacks for clothes and stopped talking for years.

Oh no, thought Marly in horror. When Uncle Beng asked, 'Well, who's next?' she ran back inside and grabbed Tuyet. 'I think your dad wants to cut your hair!'

Tuyet turned pale and put her hands up to her long black hair. 'No!' she said with dread. 'Not again! It's not fair!'

'Come on, Tuyet, it's not so bad,' coaxed Aunty Tam.

'No!'

Marly looked at Tuyet, surprised. She was sick of how Tuyet acted around adults, always so helpful, always so eager to do crappy jobs like wash vegetables and hang out the laundry. This was her chance to show that even though she was younger, she could be the bigger girl.

She turned around and bravely marched outside.

'Uncle Beng, I'll go next. But I don't want the bowl.'

'How else am I going to cut straight?' he said.

'Well, you could just start with my fringe.

And then cut my hair beneath each ear, and then all around. My mum does that.'

'You're a really bright girl. Back at the refugee camp, a girl like you would be giving haircuts for everyone!'

As Uncle Beng snipped away, Marly saw her chance to ask him something she had always wanted to know. 'Hey, Uncle Beng, how come you guys were stuck in Vietnam and Hong Kong for so long? Why didn't you try and escape?'

'I sold everything we owned to get tickets on the boat,' Uncle Beng explained.

'You mean the boat we came here on?'

'Yes. I got tickets for both our families, plus your aunty's mother. But the week we were about to leave, your aunty's mother got very sick. We had to decide what to do. Your aunty Tam couldn't leave her mother. Finally we decided that your father's family would try to make it to Australia first, and then sponsor us to come here as soon as he could. Ah, who knew it would take more than seven years.'

'But what happened to Aunty Tam's mother?'

'Oh, she died. It was very sad. Never talk about it with your aunty – she is still heartbroken. Her mother wasn't even very old. And your poor aunty Tam had to raise these two kids all by herself when they dragged me away for re-education.'

'Why didn't your family go with you too?' asked Marly.

'Oh, dear child, re-education is not what you think it might mean. It's not like sending you to school. It is more like a very hard gaol where they put you to work from early in the morning until late at night. They took me away because I was a Chinese merchant. Your aunty is Vietnamese. I saw my son for the first time only last year.'

Last year! No wonder DaWei was so close

to his mum, Marly thought. She wondered what she would be like if she had only met her father last year. There was a boy at her school, Toady, who bragged that his dad was in Pentridge Prison for armed robbery, but Marly didn't know whether he was lying to show off or not. It seemed cool that Toady had this interesting family story. Now Marly had her own interesting family members.

'All done!' said Uncle Beng. 'Now bring out that difficult cousin of yours for her haircut!'

Marly went inside and told Tuyet it was her turn. Then she looked in the mirror. She didn't look too bad, she thought. Her hair was short, even, and not too bowl-like.

That evening, lying in the small single bed pushed against the side of her parents' bed, Marly could not get to sleep. It was not her dad's snoring, but the excitement of seeing her friends at school tomorrow. She couldn't wait to tell them all about the recent unexpected changes in her family. She would explain to them that they now had a very important responsibility to look after these two poor new arrivals, who had suffered so much back in their home country.

8
First Day Back

'**O**OH, look, it's Marly!'

Marly was waving madly in the playground at Kylie and Jessica, while her cousins stood behind her.

'Oh woah,' exclaimed Jessica. 'And hey, now there's three of you!'

All summer Marly had forgotten what she looked like, because she was too busy showing her cousins new things. True, Uncle Beng had given them all short haircuts, but there weren't three of *her*.

'These are my cousins, Jermaine and Jackie.'

'No way!'

'Yes, way. It's true, they came from Hong Kong . . .' began Marly, but Kylie interrupted her.

'I mean, no way are they really named that! Jermaine and Jackie? What kind of names are those? What, are youse the Jackson 5 now?' teased Jessica.

Marly suddenly didn't want to confess that she was the one responsible for her cousins' new Australian identities. She realised that perhaps not everyone thought the Jackson 5 were cool.

'Which one is Jackie?'

Marly pointed to DaWei.

'Oh noo!' Kylie laughed. 'You have got to be kidding me. So *that* is Jermaine?' She pointed to Tuyet. 'Jermaine?'

Tuyet jolted back, as if Kylie had actually poked her.

'Hey, MyLinh, what are they talking

and laughing about?' she asked Marly in Cantonese.

'That girl is just happy to hear what your name is,' lied Marly, while Kylie kept laughing.

'Hey Marly, what did you just say? Were you speaking a different language? Don't backstab us to your cousins!' Kylie puffed out her lower lip. 'Jackie and *Jermaine*. Doesn't she realise that Jermaine is a *boy's* name?'

Marly said nothing, but she noticed Tuyet's eyes widen slightly. Tuyet didn't say anything either.

'My godmother from America sent me some My Little Ponies for Christmas,' said Jessica, holding up a purple plastic case. 'We're going over to the wooden seats to play with them. What did you get, Marly?'

'What?'

'For Christmas,' said Kylie.

For the first time, Marly realised that Kylie and Jessica spoke the same way to her as

Marly sometimes did to her cousins. Marly often had to speak slowly to her cousins who didn't know anything and even thought the toilet brush was to clean themselves with after doing number twos until she told them otherwise. But it hurt when her friends did it to her! They *knew* Marly never got anything for Christmas because her family didn't celebrate it. One year she got a plastic stocking filled with Cadbury treats from her Grade Three teacher when all of the other kids had gone home and Marly was waiting for her mother to pick her up. But aside from that, nothing. She used to wake up early on Christmas morning with the small hope that perhaps Santa might have come overnight, even though deep in her belly she knew it was like any other day for her family. After a while, she gave up this dream.

Before Marly could answer or lie, Jessica said, 'I know what you got.'

Marly braced herself for being outed by her friends.

'You got two new cousins.'

Marly's shoulders slumped with relief. 'Ha ha. You're right, Jessica. I did. They came in a set. Two for the price of one.' The moment Marly blurted this out, she felt guilty. She didn't want to be the butt of anyone's joke, so she'd picked on her cousins instead. She hoped they had not caught what she'd said about them.

Her friends laughed, but this time the tone of their laughter was different. This time it was with her, and not at her. Marly was quietly relieved – she was still part of the group.

'Do they speak English?' asked Kylie.

'A little bit,' said Marly. 'But we'll have to teach them some more. They only just got here.'

'Huh,' said Kylie without much interest. 'Well, once you're done showing them around, we'll be at the wooden benches.'

Just then the bell rang. It was time for assembly. Marly directed her cousins where to go. The whole school lined up in their different classes on the concrete lawn. Mr O'Farrell raised the Australian flag on the flagpole, and everyone began to sing the national anthem.

'Australians all let us rejoice for we are young and free . . .'

Marly looked towards Tuyet in Grade Five, and DaWei in Grade One. They were the only two not singing.

9
My Little Pony

W HEN Marly got out at lunchtime, her cousins were waiting for her at the door of her classroom.

'Wah, they sure speak really fast English here,' exclaimed Tuyet in Cantonese. 'I couldn't follow what the teacher was saying at all!'

'But you can spell words like equator and difficult,' said Marly, 'so how come your English is so bad when you talk?'

'We learned English from textbooks,' said Tuyet. 'No one actually spoke English to us in Vietnam or Hong Kong.'

'Oh.'

Marly led her cousins around the corridors, showing them the sick bay and then the Principal's office, as well as the art room and the music room. Then she led them outside to the drinking taps and toilets, the oval, the multi-purpose room where they had assemblies every Monday morning and did P.E. if it was raining, and the play equipment. They were followed by a small group of kids that grew larger as the tour progressed.

'Ning Nong Ching Chong!' yelled Jesse as he made fun of Marly's explanations to her cousins in Cantonese.

'What are they saying?' asked DaWei.

'Nothing,' muttered Marly. 'They're just making words up to sound like Chinese.'

'Why would they do that?' he asked. 'We could teach them real Chinese words.'

'Don't worry. They wouldn't want to

know,' said Marly. 'Or if they did, they'd just want to know the bad words.'

'Cha Cha Long Fong Gook!' yelled a girl named Kimberly.

'Get lost, Kimberly,' said Marly.

'Oooh! She speaks English now!' said Kimberly. 'Solly mi no spik Ingliss. Nong Pong Wah Pah?'

'Get lost, the tour's finished.'

'I'm going to tell on you,' said Kimberly. 'I'm going to tell Mr O'Farrell you're speaking another language at school.'

The group scattered away, seeing that there was no more fun to be had. Marly felt relieved. It was kind of horrible to be followed around by a massive group of kids shouting out random fake Asian words at you. When Hai had been around, the kids hadn't been such idiots. Or maybe Marly just hadn't noticed it as much, because she and Hai had both been too busy having adventures.

'Okay, so go and play now,' she commanded her cousins. 'The playground is over there.'

Tuyet and DaWei stood where they were.

Marly walked towards the oval until she got to the wooden benches where Kylie and Jessica were sitting, with the new My Little Ponies spread out. 'Hey, I'm back.'

'Everyone was watching you!' exclaimed Kylie. 'Weren't you embarrassed?'

'Nah,' lied Marly. 'I told them to get lost. Can I play?'

Kylie handed her the yellow pony. 'You can have this one. Her name is Buttercup.'

Suddenly, Marly looked up and realised that her cousins were standing there, watching her. 'Tell your friends to share their toys,' demanded Tuyet. 'I'm older, and they should respect that. They're being selfish. They have six of those tiny horses.'

'What is your cousin doing, standing over us and speaking her chinky language?' said Kylie.

'She wants you to share your toys.'

'Oh. So she thinks she can just make a grab for our My Little Ponies? Where are her My Little Ponies to share, huh?'

'She doesn't mean it like that,' protested Marly, but she could also see it from Jessica and Kylie's side. You shouldn't have to share your stuff if you didn't want to, especially to people you might not like. Oh, if only Tuyet would show them how fun she was, how good she was at making up stories, how she could use boring things like lolly wrappers and leaves and hard berries and seeds and nutshells to make bowls and clothes and amazing things for toys. If only she could – but they couldn't even understand a single word that came out of Tuyet's mouth. And Tuyet was pretty fierce when she wanted to be.

Kylie, who was used to being the most popular girl in school, was not scared. 'Yes, Jermajesty.'

Jessica cackled. 'Whatever you say, Jermajesty! Ha ha, good one, Kylie!'

Tuyet glared at them, but they ignored her and went back to playing with their My Little Ponies.

Marly turned to her cousins. 'You both better go and find something else to do,' she told them.

'But you're supposed to play with us!' protested DaWei.

'Go away! You need to find your own friends,' said Marly.

'Oh no. There you go, talking that weird talk again, Marly!' said Kylie.

As her cousins sadly walked away, Marly knew she had started something terrible. She felt a stab of guilt, because they reminded her of when she'd first started school, before she met Hai. At least her cousins weren't alone, she told herself. At least they had each other. If Marly joined them, all her hard work at belonging would be completely wasted – she'd just be another ching-chong who other kids and new teachers might think couldn't even speak English properly.

She knew that if her cousins dobbed on her at home, she would be in big trouble. But she couldn't help it. It was only in the middle of last year that Kylie and Jessica let her hang around with them, after Mrs Horton read them a story about a boy who escaped the war in Vietnam and came on a boat to Australia. For about a week, they were fascinated by the fact that Marly had come to Australia by boat as well, and kept hounding her for details.

Marly told them about seasickness, pirates with eye patches and gimpy legs, hungry sharks, and a family of dolphins. She had only been two years old on the boat and couldn't really remember very much, so she made it up. Then she suggested they play pirates and shipwreck, and that was how the friendship began.

For the first time, Marly had felt accepted at school by the other kids, and more than that, liked for her imagination. It was only later, when Kylie started getting toys sent to her from her godmother in America, that Marly's made-up games started to become a little stale.

She asked Kylie, 'Hey, what would happen if you told your parents that you didn't want Richard hanging around you all the time?' Richard was Kylie's six-year-old brother.

'Why would he hang around me? He's got his own friends. He wouldn't be caught dead near me and my things.'

Marly didn't particularly like playing with those stupid ponies either, but she wasn't about to say that now. 'But just say he really wanted to,' she insisted.

'Then my parents would tell him to leave me alone.'

This made Marly certain of what a crazy,

unfair family she had. She saw her cousins all the time at home, so why couldn't they understand that she needed her own friends at school?

Every lunchtime Marly's cousins kept appearing at the wooden benches where she and her friends played, and every lunchtime Marly had to tell them to get lost.

'But I have your lunch!' said Tuyet. She handed Marly a blue plastic container. It made a rattling noise. She also gave Marly a metal drinking flask.

'No, Tuyet, I already ate my lunch,' Marly lied. She had forgotten her lunch that morning, she'd been so eager to walk to school ahead of her cousins.

'But it's your favourite lunch. Look!' Tuyet peeled open the plastic lid of the container.

'Oh, did you just see that?' exclaimed

Jessica. 'Coco Pops! She brought you Coco Pops for lunch!'

'Crazy, crazy Jermajesty. Where's the milk?' Kylie joked.

Tuyet pointed to the metal flask. 'In there.' She even handed Marly a spoon.

'Oh my goodness,' laughed Jessica. 'I can't believe it! This is too funny!'

'Go away, Tuyet! I don't want it!'

'Ooh, there you go speaking in chink again,' said Jessica.

Tuyet looked at Marly and Marly knew that she understood and wanted to say something back to Jessica, but she didn't. 'Come on brother, let's go,' she said. They turned and walked away.

Marly looked at the opened container of Coco Pops. She was hungry, but not hungry enough to humiliate herself.

'Neiigghh!' said Kylie's My Little Pony Blue Belle as she dug her nose into Marly's meal. Jessica made her pony join in too. 'Come on, horseys, feed time! Ooh!' exclaimed Kylie, 'I'm going to take a bath in oats.' She dumped her My Little Pony in the container and made it smoosh around. 'This is such fun!'

There was no way Marly was going to be able to eat her Coco Pops now, so she did the same with Buttercup. As the other girls laughed, Marly pretended not to notice her cousins standing a little way off, watching in horror at what to them was a waste of perfectly good food.

10
Tuyet the Genius

*D*ON'T walk so close to me,' demanded Marly.

'We have to go home together. We live in the same house, remember?' said Tuyet.

'But you don't have to walk so close!'

Every afternoon when they walked out the school gate and down the first three streets of the neighbourhood, Marly made sure she walked in front of her cousins while Tuyet and DaWei walked behind her, yelling, 'You can't trick them, you stupid girl! We look alike – they know we are with you!'

This made Marly really mad.

'I'm meant to look out for you, I'm your older cousin,' said Tuyet.

'You're not even that much older than me! Two years, big deal.' Something had shifted in Marly. The more effort her cousins made to be close to her at school, the more embarrassed she felt for them.

Why are they trying to steal me away? Marly thought angrily. They're just trying to make me into the girl I was three years ago with Hai, the crazy, tree-climbing, rock-tossing tomboy who chose not to speak English at school. Marly remembered the looks of disapproval from teachers, who constantly reminded her to 'Speak English, Marly! You're in Australia now!' And the students who laughed because her best friend was a boy who used a sock as a pencilcase.

The days grew hotter and hotter. After school the three of them would sit listlessly in front of the television. Marly and DaWei didn't even play together outside anymore. Their school lives had changed their home lives. They would sit silently and watch the children's programs on the ABC. At night, all the programs were constantly interrupted by updates about the bushfires burning all around Melbourne.

'The worst in the history of the state,' the news reporter said grimly one Wednesday.

'Yes,' agreed Uncle Beng. 'Terrible things can happen anywhere. Even so close to home. Where's Tuyet?'

'In the back shed,' replied Marly.

'What is she doing there?' asked Uncle Beng. Marly didn't know, so she went to find out.

'Can I help you, Aunty?' asked Tuyet, standing by Marly's mother's sewing machine. It was boiling in the back shed and Aunty Tam was even ironing shirts.

'I suppose you could, Tuyet. I have to go and get some dinner ready before your dad gets home.' Marly's mother got out of her seat, and Tuyet took her place and started the machine. Marly couldn't believe it!

'How come she gets to help sew?' complained Marly.

'She's capable and sensible. See what a straight line she is sewing.'

The praise tipped Marly over the edge. 'It's not fair, you never let me do anything! If you'd let me sew I could do that!'

'You're too easily distracted, Marlin,' said her mother. 'Look at your cousin. She knows how to be still.'

Marly glared at Tuyet sitting there so smug, sewing perfect lines. Being still was for trees. Being still was for very fat grannies who sat in their rocking chairs drinking tea and eating Tic Toc biscuits from a packet.

'When did you learn how to sew anyway?'

Marly asked her cousin.

'While you and DaWei were outside mucking about, I asked your mum to teach me.'

Marly turned to her aunty Tam. She didn't really want to iron, but she offered anyway. 'Hey Aunty, can I help *you*?'

Aunty Tam looked down at the shirt on the ironing board that had taken them three hours to make. 'Uhh, sweet pup, maybe you could help your mum make some dinner?' she suggested.

'No fair!' cried Marly as she stormed back into the house. She didn't want to help anyone now. She would only be in the way, not like perfect Tuyet. She went back and sat in front of the television, hoping that something good would come on, like the video clip to Michael Jackson's 'Thriller' or 'Beat It', which sometimes played in between TV programs.

DaWei bounded in with a furry creature in

his hands. 'Look at this!' he said.

'Where'd you get a new toy?' demanded Marly. Then she realised that it wasn't new at all. It was her Duracell bunny, but he looked like a different creature. Tuyet had sewn him a smart new outfit, complete with a stripy shirt and overalls held together by two buttons. She'd removed his drum and drumsticks, and attached a small bouncy ball on a thin elastic thread between his paws.

She pretended not to be impressed and turned back to the television just as her father walked in.

'Excuse me, Uncle, but do you have those big round batteries?' Tuyet asked Marly's dad sweetly.

'What size?' he replied. 'Why do you need them for?'

DaWei held up the bunny.

'Wah, who got you a new toy?'

'It's MyLinh's old bunny,' said DaWei.

'See? My sister fixed it.'

Marly's father took the bunny and looked at it closely. 'This is amazing,' he said. 'Let's find those batteries!'

Marly ground her teeth and concentrated on the television as her dad found two C-cell batteries from an old radio, lifted up bunny's overall leg, and inserted them in the side. Suddenly, Duracell bunny came to life, but instead of banging on a drum he was bouncing a red rubber ball from one paw to the other.

'Wah, this is just incredible,' said her dad. 'Ay, Beng, come and have a look at this!'

Uncle Beng came over. 'Oh, she's good with her hands,' he said. 'She's always doing stuff like this.'

'This is genius,' exclaimed Marly's dad. 'An entirely new invention! If only Marly could create such wonders, instead of wrecking existing ones.'

Marly ignored them as her mother and aunty appeared, hot and sweaty, to see what all the fuss was about.

'Look at this, Diep,' said Marly's dad. 'This girl is talented. Her talent will blow you away.'

'Wah!' exclaimed Marly's mum.

Then to Uncle Beng he said, 'Brother, your daughter could be anything she wants! An engineer. An inventor. A mechanic. A designer. Anything. Look at the physics of this thing!'

Marly was so angry now she felt ill. If someone had put a bowl of chocolate ice-cream in front of her at that very moment, she didn't think she'd have been able to eat a single spoonful. Marly knew that her father hoped that she would become an engineer one day in the future, because he used to be an engineer in Vietnam.

'What about DaWei?' asked Marly's uncle, which Marly thought was a strange question to ask. 'Do you think he shows talent, brother?'

'Too early to say,' said Marly's father. 'But there may be hope for him if he turns out anything like his sister.'

'I wish DaWei was more like his sister,' Marly overheard her uncle muttering to her aunty. 'All that talent is wasted on a girl. All she needs to know how to do is boil a good pot of rice.'

Marly was waiting for her aunty to burst out laughing at this joke, but no laughter came. They were serious!

Marly looked at DaWei happily playing with the bunny and Tuyet watching silently from the doorway. Just a moment ago Tuyet's face had been flushed with pride, but now it was flushed in a bad way. It was the same way Marly's face heated up when she was trying not to cry. For a moment, Marly felt very sorry for her cousin.

11
Bad Names

UYET may have been a genius at recycling old toys, but at school Marly got to play with the latest ones. Last year, Jessica had Pink & Pretty Barbie while Kylie had Twirly Curls Barbie, so they had let Marly play with Great Shape Ken. Marly made him do cool things – climb cliffs (the large rock near the drinking taps) to rescue one of them, walk on very high and narrow ledges on skyscrapers (the school barbeque), and jump out of the sky with nothing but a Twisties packet parachute. The best thing of all was that Ken could do all these amazing tricks and the Barbies would have to say, 'Ooh, wow, Ken, you are so amazing. Thank you for saving our lives.'

'You know what, Marly,' Kylie said out of the blue one day, 'you do a great Ken voice. You don't even have an accent. I don't see you as chinky.'

Marly knew exactly what 'chinky' meant. It meant not speaking English, and taking great delight in eating Coco Pops for lunch, *dry*, without even caring that they were a breakfast food. It meant jabbering in Cantonese all the time so no one could understand what you were saying or if you were talking about them behind their back. It meant saving your Glad Wrap so you could blow it into a big plastic bubble for your brother to pop. It meant searching the schoolyard at lunchtime for dropped lollies.

'I don't even care that you're Asian,' added Jessica. 'In fact, most of the time I forget that you are. You're just like us, Marly.'

That was all Marly needed to hear. She glowed with happiness.

'Wow, Barbies, youse look beautiful,' Marly told them, even though she really thought they looked demented.

Despite everything at school, Tuyet and DaWei seemed to be happy. Marly could not understand how they were. When she had been picked on in Grade Two for peeing her pants, the other kids had teased her terribly at recess. For two whole weeks she'd tried not to drink anything at school so she wouldn't need to go to the toilet. And when she'd gone home, she'd skulked around the house miserably, the scene running like a constant cassette-tape loop in her brain.

But what happened at school just didn't seem to affect her cousins.

One evening after dinner, the whole family watched Michael Jackson on television. He was on a special show called 'Motown 25', celebrating twenty-five years of their music company. His brothers were talented and handsome, but Michael was something else altogether. He had a tendril of curly hair hanging down the middle of his forehead, like a grapevine. He wore a black hat and one single white sequinned glove. His jacket shimmered like a road at night beneath the moon. He sang a song about a girl named Billie Jean.

And he did something amazing. After spinning like an ice skater without skates, leaping on his toes and a few crazy high kicks, he glided backwards as if he were on a horizontal escalator.

Her whole family went 'Wahhh' over this nifty move. Aunty Tam looked baffled and asked, 'But why is he wearing a lady's jacket and only one glove?'

'It's not fair!' complained DaWei after the show. 'Why didn't you name me Michael instead?'

'You *wanted* to be Jackie,' said Marly. And anyway, Michael was too special. Marly would never call anyone else that. She sat there, aglow with happiness over the magic of what she'd just seen.

'You!' Tuyet suddenly exploded. 'You named me after that man with the purple shoes that matched his guitar!' The reality of her name had not sunk in for Tuyet until now. 'The teacher at the school thought I was German! "German? Gerrr-man?" she called out on the first day. "German Vo?" When I realised it was me and answered, she said, "What are you? A European car?"'

Marly couldn't help smirking. She had no idea what a European car was, but it was pretty funny. She knew that the other kids would have done the same. She glanced at her dad, who was also smirking.

'Come on, brother, you have to admit, that's a little funny,' he said to his elder brother. 'It's just a joke.'

'We're sorry we don't get your jokes,' said Uncle Beng angrily. 'We are not as educated as you are, remember? We didn't get the chance to finish high school. I had to take care of the family business.'

Tuyet started sniffing loudly, and then Aunty Tam began to get teary too. Soon enough, even DaWei was crying.

'You see?' retorted Uncle Beng. 'You see what a terrible thing your daughter has done to my trusting children? She has given them black man names!'

'Don't be so dramatic,' said Marly's father. 'Marly picked a group of popular, talented musicians. At least Jermaine's named after the most handsome member!'

'Don't kid around with me!' warned Uncle

Beng, his voice getting louder.

'But I'm not. I let Marly pick her own name from that same group! Of course, at the time I had no idea they were a group of young *men . . .*'

'Enough!' This time Uncle Beng was really shouting. 'You see, Duong, that is why your daughter is the way she is. Impertinent. Spoilt. She can't sit still because you let her run around all the time and jump on our bed when we're not home! No sense of respect for her elders. Just like you.'

Marly's father didn't usually get angry, but Marly could see him clamping his jaw very tightly shut so that he would not say what was on his mind. She thought how strange it was that her father was acting this way around his brother, when ordinarily, if one of his friends drank a bit too much VB and started to say things that irked him, he would be able to give them a piece of his mind.

'You watch it,' he'd often say to his friends. 'Or I'm going to kick you so hard that by the time you stop rolling, your clothes will be out of fashion!'

Of course, Marly's dad meant this as a joke. He'd never kick anyone. But it seemed that you could never joke with Uncle Beng. He looked like he hadn't smiled in thirty years.

'We sacrificed a lot to get you and your family to Australia first,' said Uncle Beng. 'The least you can do is have your kid show my kids a little more respect!'

'She doesn't even want to know us at school!' wailed Tuyet. 'She ignores us and pretends that we aren't related.'

Marly's mum turned towards her. 'Is this true?'

Marly couldn't help herself. 'They ruin everything!' she hollered.

Suddenly, Marly's mum dragged her up by her elbow and gave her a big smack on her bum. Marly howled even louder. The smack didn't really hurt that much, but she needed to pretend that it did, because she knew how these things worked. If you didn't show enough misery, you'd get more smacks. 'Aooowwww!' wailed Marly.

'Apologise to your cousins now,' demanded her mother.

'I'm sorry Tuyet! Sorry, DaWei!'

But deep inside, Marly wasn't really sorry. She was very angry. Her parents just didn't understand anything about wanting to fit in and not being lumped as one of the only three Asian kids at school.

'Family must always stick together,' her father told her.

12
Bored with Barbies

ARLY was making Ken do the Moonwalk at school. She'd learned this was what Michael Jackson called his backwards–walking dance move. Marly liked how Great Shape Ken had flat feet, unlike the tiptoeing Barbies whose feet reminded Marly of cartoon characters. Whenever they were up to no good, Sylvester the Cat and Elmer Fudd would sneak around corners on their toes to avoid being seen. There was something untrustworthy like that about the Barbies. They were quiet and elegant, but Marly got the feeling that they would pounce on you when you least expected it.

'Stop mucking about with Ken,' said Kylie. 'We need T.C. to judge which one of us looks better for the Crystal Ball.'

T.C. was what they called the old Twirly Curls Barbie.

Marly thought it was ridiculous. The two other Barbies were going to a ball in the 'Crystal Cave', a hollow in a large rock where it would be completely dark and probably stinky with bird poo, and they were dressed in lace outfits and high heels. They stood there, waiting for T.C. to judge their random beauty contest. Marly made T.C. just point to the nearest one. 'Her,' she said, 'I pick her.'

'Ha!' gloated Jessica. 'I win!'

'That's not fair!' protested Kylie. Then she said to Marly, 'You're not even trying, are you?'

'Yes, I am,' said Marly.

'Fine.' Kylie took both dolls and hid them behind her back. 'Now you have to guess what colour . . .'

'I know, I know,' sighed Marly. 'I have to guess what colour dresses they were wearing. Yours was wearing some kind of puffy purple thing.'

'No,' said Jessica. 'What colour *earrings* were they both wearing?'

'I don't know!' Marly was sick of this game. 'I really don't want to play with Twirly Curls Barbie. I was happy with Ken.'

'You see, Kylie? She's ruining it for us!' Marly knew that Jessica was just trying to distract Kylie from rubbing it in that she had won the beauty contest. 'You've let her play with your doll that she was eyeing off all last year, and she doesn't want to anymore.'

Kylie's eyes glowed dangerously like matches and Marly knew she was close to ending their friendship.

'Fine then,' said Kylie, 'if Marly doesn't want her, we'll throw her away.' She grabbed Twirly Curls Barbie by the legs, and walked towards the nearest rubbish bin.

'Wait! What are you doing?' said Marly, running towards her. 'Don't be stupid, Kylie!' Even though Marly didn't particularly like Twirly Curls Barbie, she didn't want her to end up buried among apple cores and Zooper Dooper Wrappers and half-eaten Vegemite sandwiches.

But she was too late. Kylie flung the Barbie into the bin as Jessica looked sadly on.

'Wait! You can't just leave her there!' protested Marly.

'What are you, Marly? A bin scab?' asked Jessica.

'Yeah, Marly, do you fish things out of bins and play with them? Like your cousins?' They walked back to their dolls.

Marly didn't say a word as she joined her

friends. She couldn't believe that they had chucked out a perfectly good toy. It was a crime.

'Okay, where were we up to?' asked Kylie. 'Oh! I remember! Ken was going to take Dream Date Barbie out to get married in Mildura. So come on, Ken! Get in the convertible and drive over to her house!'

Marly really hated this game now, but she had no choice but to continue. In the distance she could see her cousins, walking by themselves as usual, searching the oval for dropped lollies and hidden treasure. It seemed to Marly that they were having more fun than she ever would with her friends.

What was worse, her cousins had stopped talking to her at school. They let her walk home by herself in front of them, while they laughed and told jokes in Cantonese.

At home, Tuyet and DaWei stuck closely together like they had when they'd first arrived, blocking Marly out. With such a full house, it was strange that Marly felt even lonelier than she ever had before.

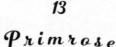

13

Primrose

*A*T home, Marly's mum and aunty were picking the ends off bean sprouts and Tuyet was roasting peanuts in a frying pan.

'Not fair,' complained Marly, 'you never let me do that.'

'Come here and you can help wash the spinach,' coaxed her aunty.

'But that's no fun.' It was no fun being all good and helpful because you got stuck with all the boring jobs, thought Marly, unlike Tuyet. The adults seemed to prefer her, she thought sullenly. She ignored the fact that

Tuyet had spent months doing the boring jobs and had only just been allowed to start cooking on the stove.

'Look,' Tuyet said to Marly after dinner, when they were sitting on the sofa watching television. She held out a familiar object in front of Marly's face.

It was Twirly Curls Barbie. Tuyet had sewed a beautiful ballgown for her out of a piece of pink satin she must have found in the school Art Room scraps pile. She'd carefully peeled off all the gold stars she'd received on her worksheets and stuck them on the dress. Where the doll's hair had once been tangled into five different plaits, it was now wavy and soft from shampoo and conditioning. And out of the gold foil that looked like it was from the lid of a Nutella jar, Tuyet had made a crown.

T.C. looked like a new doll now, and even though she'd never admit it, Marly was pleased that Tuyet had fished her out of the bin and given her a new life. She knew Tuyet would take care of Twirly Curls Barbie much better than Kylie. Marly didn't ask her cousin where she got her new toy from. She just said, casually, 'Nice doll. What's her name?'

'Primrose.'

'Primrose? Where on earth did you come up with a name like that?' exclaimed Marly.

'Do you want to play with her?' Tuyet offered generously

Marly shuddered. She didn't ever want to see T.C. again. 'No thanks.'

Marly decided she had to get Kylie and Jessica to do something else at lunchtimes other than play Barbies or she would go crazy. She suggested jumping rope, playing elastics, looking for insects to keep in jars, even pouring bottles of water into the sandpit to make quicksand for the My Little Ponies. But it was no use – Kylie and Jessica stuck to the Barbies, even when Kane walked past them all one day and said, 'Hey, aren't you a little too old for dolls?'

They used the Barbies to say things to each other that they wouldn't dare say in real life. And they used Marly to come between them when things started getting nasty, like when Kylie's Dream Date Barbie said to Jessica's Pink Barbie, 'How come you're wearing your pyjamas out?' Or when Pink Barbie told Dream Date that her face was ugly.

When this happened, Marly would quickly distract them with Ken. Ken would make a bad joke, or trapeze through the air to save the distressed damsel and karate-kick the other Barbie in the face.

'What a horrible thing to do!' they would say to Marly, distracted, and everything would be forgotten.

One day, as Marly was trying to get Dream
Date out of trouble – she had fallen down a
deep ravine and could not get up and would
not take off her clumsy long wraparound
skirt to use as a lasso – Marly saw Tuyet
approaching.

Oh no, thought Marly, here comes real
trouble.

'Can I play?' asked Tuyet.

'Sorry, Jermajesty,' said Kylie, 'but you need
a Barbie.'

'I got a Barbie.' Tuyet took Primrose from
her Cathay Pacific bag. 'I also got Barbie
clothes.' She pulled out a white tulle wedding
dress, a peasant blouse, an off-the-shoulder
T-shirt, and some tiny shorts.

'Woah, that's really cool,' said Jessica. 'I've
never seen a doll with so many clothes before.
Did they all come in the same box?'

'What kind of Barbie is she?' asked Kylie
suspiciously.

'Huh?'

Marly was embarrassed that her cousin did not yet know how to say 'Pardon?' or 'I'm sorry, what did you say?'

'I mean, is she a Crystal Barbie? Or a Bridal Barbie? Or what?'

'She Pimross.'

'Huh?'

'She means Primrose,' explained Marly.

'Primrose Barbie? Never heard of that before. What does she do?' asked Jessica.

'Huh?'

'That's my doll!' cried Kylie suddenly. 'She stole my doll!'

'Don't be a sook, Kylie,' said Marly. 'You chucked her out, remember?'

'No! It's not fair! I didn't say *she* could have her! I want her back!'

'But she's not yours anymore, you chucked her out,' Marly repeated.

'She stole my doll!' hollered Kylie.

Soon, a small group of kids had gathered around.

'It mine,' said Tuyet. 'I find her.'

'Where, then?' asked Kane.

'In the . . .' began Tuyet, and then she must have realised it was not a good idea to tell them exactly where. 'Over there.' She pointed in the direction of the school oval.

'And where did you lose it?' Kane asked Kylie.

'I don't know,' Kylie lied. 'Somewhere over there.' She also pointed at the oval. 'She's my favourite doll. I've had her since I was eight.' A tear rolled out of Kylie's big green eyes.

Oh come on, thought Marly, you've only had her for one year, and it's your own fault for chucking her away. Marly knew she should do something. She should speak up, because her cousin couldn't speak for herself without the other kids making fun of her or pulling up their eyelid corners and yelling 'ching chong, ching chong!' She had to tell the truth. She took a deep breath.

'She stole it from Kylie!' accused Jessica.

'No, you stupid derbrain,' Marly finally exploded. 'You know she didn't. Kylie chucked it in the bin. She chucked it in the bin over there!'

Everyone looked in the direction where Marly was pointing.

'You chucked her in the bin?' asked Kimberly in disbelief.

'But how come it doesn't look dirty? How come the doll is still so new?' asked Kane.

'Because I didn't chuck her in the bin – *she* stole her from me!' repeated Kylie. She was crying now.

'Nooo,' said Tuyet. 'I never stole. I clin eet.'

'My cousin found the stupid doll and cleaned it and made the dress for her,' said Marly. 'Have a look if you don't believe me.' She pulled the doll out of bewildered Tuyet's hands, and thrust it at Kane. Kimberly, who believed she was more of an expert at sussing these things out, took it from him. She examined the doll carefully.

'You're a liar, Marly,' she finally said. 'This dress is made by a machine. I know because my aunty Gwen has one at her house. That's why the stitches are so neat. It's made by an adult. There is no way *she'* – and here, Kimberly jabbed the doll at Tuyet's direction – 'no way that she could make something like this.'

'But she can!' said Marly. 'She can sew!'

'Liar. You don't have to stick up for your cousin. We know she's a thief. Youse are all thieves. My mum says the chinks come here and steal jobs.'

It was that word that did it. Marly's face started to burn, and her heart was like an exploding water bomb in her chest. She hurled herself at Kimberly, and grabbed at her hair with one hand, taking in a handful of those perfect brown ringlets, and snatched Tuyet's doll with the other. She let go and gave it back to Tuyet. Kimberly started howling. 'Waahhhh!' she cried. 'You pulled my hair!'

Kane made a grab for Marly but she quickly stepped back. She held her hands like knives in front of her face and chest. 'I know kung fu,' she said. 'Hwaaah!'

'What the . . . '

'Karate!' Marly yelled, realising they might not know what kung fu was, that they might have thought it was the same as ching-chong. 'Karate! Fighting with bare hands! We invented the Chinese burn! We invented the death of a thousand cuts! Hwaaah!' She rolled her hands round and round, hoping that it would look like she was ready to slice someone into a couple of salami chunks.

'You are crazy,' muttered Kane, but he backed away from Marly.

Marly felt victorious.

'Hwaaah!' she screeched again.

'What is going on here?'

It was Mrs Louden, their teacher. She looked around and saw Kimberly and Kylie in tears, Tuyet holding a Barbie doll and snivelling, and Marly yelling like a hyena.

Kylie piped up between tears, 'Miss, Miss, she stole my Barbie!' She pointed a finger at Tuyet, who clutched the doll closer to her chest.

'Did not! You throw in rubbiss. I find her.'

Mrs Louden looked at Tuyet long and hard. 'Is this true?'

'Yes.'

She then turned to Kylie and looked at her long and hard too. 'Is that true, Kylie? Did you throw this doll away in the bin? Now, don't lie to me.'

Kylie looked at the ground, and murmured, 'But it was only a joke.'

'She left it in there all day and didn't go

back to get it,' said Marly. 'I saw.'

Tuyet held onto the doll so tightly that her knuckles were white.

'Let me have a look at that,' said Mrs Louden, and took the doll from Tuyet.

'Miss, Miss, she's a liar!' said Kimberly. 'She said that she made the doll's clothes herself too!'

Mrs Louden turned the doll around in her hands and looked at the dress with the carefully stuck-on gold stars, the crown and the clean hair. 'Good job, Tuyet,' she said, handing Primrose back to her. 'Lovely stitching.'

Kylie's mouth was a big bewildered O. So was Jessica's.

'Next time,' Mrs Louden said to Kylie, 'pay more respect to your things instead of throwing them away.'

When Mrs Louden walked away, Jessica said loudly, 'I hate her!' Kylie started to cry again.

At that moment, Marly realised how much she liked Mrs Louden. She was not only good and kind, but she was fair.

'Finders Keepers, Kylie!' gloated Marly, this time not caring what her friends thought.

Suddenly, Jessica grabbed the doll from Tuyet's surprised hands. 'I don't care what the teacher says, this belongs to Kylie!' Jessica ripped the lovely pink satin gown from Barbie, squished her tinfoil crown with one hand, and handed the doll back to Kylie. 'Here, it's yours.'

Kylie took the doll back, but without its new dress, it was just her old Barbie again in the fading yellow swimsuit, the one she didn't want in the first place. Everyone could see this. Stupid, greedy Kylie, Marly thought angrily, she's made a big deal out of nothing.

To hide her embarrassment, Kylie gave a sharp tug and pulled Barbie's head off. She threw the two parts of the doll down at

Tuyet's feet. 'You can have it,' she said. 'I don't want it back. It's got your germs on it. Gross.' She nodded at Jessica and the two girls walked away in a huff.

The other kids started to move away. The action was over.

Marly looked at her teary cousin, with the broken doll at her feet. She didn't care who was watching. She bent down, picked up Barbie and popped her head back onto her body. She handed it back to Tuyet.

'Thanks,' sniffed her cousin.

Marly felt free. She didn't care what Kylie and Jessica thought of her anymore.

'Let's walk home together,' she told her cousins when the bell rang for the end of lunchtime.

$\mathcal{I}$T seemed that Tuyet and DaWei weren't too concerned about what anyone else thought of them either. It was as if the Barbie incident had never happened. Marly's mum had given Tuyet a length of elastic from her sewing supplies, and the following day at lunchtime, Tuyet tied the elastic in a loop around two empty metal bicycle stands, while DaWei stood at the other end with the elastic stretched around his knees. Marly found them taking it in turns to jump in and out of the elastic, and to hold the end.

'You might want an extra person to hold the other end so you don't need to tie it to the bike rack,' she suggested. 'Maybe I could hold it for you.' Without a word, Tuyet untied the elastic from the bike rack, and re-looped it around Marly's legs. And this was how Marly came to join her cousins at lunchtime.

She hunted with them on the oval, around and around, looking for lost treasure. Many times they would find one or two dropped wrapped lollies, and one lucky lunch they even found a dollar which they took to the canteen and bought five Redskins with.

Another lunchtime Marly suggested that they empty water bottles out into the sandpit to make quicksand. Soon, a corner of the sandpit was filled with light brown sludge that they stirred and stirred. Tuyet made little people out of twigs and hard inedible purple plums that dropped into the playground from a neighbouring tree, and they played

Armies in the War. Tuyet made little chairs and tables out of Prima boxes, and rings out of Coke pulls. What was incredible to Marly was that they always found something in the playground to play with.

Every time Marly and her cousins walked past Kylie and Jessica, Marly noticed a new addition to the group – Kimberly. But they were doing the exact same thing as always, playing Barbies, and Marly secretly gloated that there was no way Kimberly, with her sooky ways and her high voice, would make as good a Ken as Marly had been.

Marly also realised that all the while she had been playing with Ken – making him go on adventures, telling jokes and creating a fearless character – she was being herself through a small plastic doll, when now, with her cousins, she could be herself all the time.

The other kids left Marly and her cousins alone at lunchtime, but strangely enough,

Marly didn't mind. She felt like she and her cousins were marooned on their own little island, but she had chosen it, and she was happy. They even had their own language – Cantonese – that no one else in the school could understand. Whenever Kane or Billy or Chantal walked by and called them names, Marly and Tuyet and DaWei would hurl back worse ones in Cantonese and laugh.

At home, the adults started to comment on Marly's change in attitude.

'You're really helpful now,' said Aunty Tam when Marly offered to hang out the washing with Tuyet.

'You're so much more focused,' marvelled Marly's dad, watching as Tuyet showed Marly how to make a spinning top for DaWei with an old metal wheel from a toy car.

Marly glowed at their praise. It felt good to be helpful.

'How do you know how to make this stuff?' she asked Tuyet in awe one day.

Tuyet shrugged. 'Hong Kong was a big city full of poster ads about the latest cool gadgets and toys and stuff. But we were stuck in the refugee camp and I had to look after mum and DaWei. I wanted him to have toys so I collected old clothes and broken clocks and made them myself.'

Marly began to realise that her cousin had never been a suck-up, that she'd always just been serious and responsible. Tuyet had never gloated about all the stuff she knew, and she was always patient. 'Here,' said Tuyet, handing Marly the wheel attached to a wooden chopstick. 'Give it a spin.'

Things continued like this for three more blissful weeks, although Marly didn't see her cousins much over the weekends. They were always out with Uncle Beng and Aunty Tam visiting friends who had arrived in Australia earlier and now lived in the Commission flats.

The Commission flats were buildings that rose so high they seemed to poke the sky. Aunty Tam liked them because they reminded her of the apartments of wealthy people in Hong Kong. She'd never been inside a Hong Kong apartment, of course, but she claimed they had the same black-and-white floors and modern kitchens, and bathrooms that had a shower on top of a bathtub and no squat toilet. To her, these were luxury.

When they came back, their eyes were filled with awe over all the rooms that could one day be theirs, and all the spaces they could keep their things.

Then, one day, they got it. A place of their own.

'It's on the seventeenth floor,' said Tuyet, grinning. 'And it has its own playground.

You can come over and play any time you want.'

Marly felt a small stab of the old jealousy – she was supposed to be the one giving her poor cousins all the stuff they never had, not the other way around!

But deeper than that was another strange feeling: an aching empty sort of feeling. She had always known that her cousins would not be staying with them forever, but while they were around, it felt as if she had her own siblings – annoying at times, but often full of unexpected laughs.

She'd started off with such good intentions to show her cousins around, but when they'd arrived and she'd realised how embarrassing they were, Marly had wanted nothing to do with them. She had been so mean to them.

And now, just when she'd realised she felt much happier being with them than with her other supposed friends, they were leaving.

And going to a new school as well – one that was closer to their new home.

She watched sadly as her cousins prepared to leave.

Moving weekend was a day filled with sunlight and blue sky. Aunty Tam and Uncle Beng helped Marly's parents clean the house. Finally, they took down the navy curtains with the polka dots. When the curtains came down, Marly could see that her uncle's family had already packed their bags. They had also stripped the bed so it was just a bare mattress again.

Marly gave Tuyet the Rubik's cube to take with her, and DaWei the Duracell bunny. She watched as Tuyet fiddled with the cube and in only a couple of minutes had the colours lined up on each side.

'Back at the camp,' Tuyet said, 'we spent

years in one room. There wasn't very much to do, and one time the Red Cross gave me a Rubik's cube as a Christmas present. I spent months trying to work it out.'

Marly had never spent months trying to work out one simple problem. When the cube had gotten too difficult, she had just tossed it aside and played with her other toys. When Duracell bunny got a broken drumstick, she'd just tossed him aside too. She'd never stuck with something. Instead of showing her friends who she really was, she'd been so scared of losing them that she'd just worked on getting rid of her cousins, which was easier.

Tuyet and DaWei, on the other hand, had turned up every afternoon to walk home with her after school. Even when she walked in front of them and pretended they weren't there. They'd brought her lunch when she had forgotten it. And they'd let her join in when they saw she had lost her friends. They understood that family always stuck together.

She could not imagine going to school on Monday morning and being alone again at recess. But Marly knew she was tough, she would sort something out.

'That's it then,' Marly's dad said after they had loaded all their suitcases in the car. 'Say goodbye to your cousins, Marly.'

'Don't be ridiculous,' scoffed Marly's mum. 'This isn't a serious farewell! They're just moving fifteen minutes' drive away! They'll still all see each other every weekend when Tam comes to help me sew.'

Marly was very relieved.

'See you later, Germainn and Jacky!' Marly said, for old times' sake.

'Hey!' said Tuyet. 'Just you wait. I'm going to change my name when I get to my new school.'

'Not me,' said DaWei. 'I like Jackie.'

'What will you change your name to?'

Marly asked Tuyet.

'Primrose.'

You have got to be kidding me, that's almost as bad as Rapunzel, thought Marly. But over the past few months, she had learned not to blurt out the first thing she thought.

'What about Rosie?' she said instead.

'Rosie,' Tuyet repeated thoughtfully. 'I like that. Maybe I will. Here. This is for you.' She gave Marly something in a white plastic bag. When Marly opened it, she saw that it was the elastic they played with at lunchtimes.

'But I can't play with this by myself!' Marly protested.

'I guess you'll have to make some new friends again, then, ay?'

Marly smiled. She supposed that she would, when she went back to school. But that was tomorrow. Now, she watched her father drive her uncle, aunty and cousins to their new flat. She was back to being an only child again, with all the space in her house back. Wasn't that what she'd always wanted?

She went back inside and kneeled on the floor to help her mother peel the duct tape from the shower curtains. 'What will you do with these now, Mum?' she asked.

'We'll fold them carefully and put them in the garage,' her mother told her. 'In case we need them again.'

Marly smiled – her mother could never throw anything away.

'You know,' Marly suggested, 'you could always put these curtains back to good use.'

'Oh?' asked her mum. 'And how would I do that?'

'Well, I have a good idea. You could make me my own room.'

Her mother stopped peeling the duct tape. 'Maybe that is a good idea,' she said. 'You've had to share so much for so long. We'll wait until your father gets home and see if he can help me re-hang the curtain rod. In the meantime, where's the tape? We'd better stick it together again.'

This time, Marly did not muck about. She did not jump on the bed or pretend that the curtains were an oversized calculator or Atari game. She got right down to work.

HOW I BECAME AN AUSTRALIAN GIRL

Alice Pung

My parents were born in Cambodia. My mum worked in a plastic bag factory when she was only 13 years old, and my dad's family owned that factory. That's how my parents met!

In 1975 there was a war in Cambodia and my parents were separated. Four years later they met again in Vietnam, and romance blossomed. In December 1980, my parents came as refugees by boat to Australia. I was born a month later. Dad named me Alice, because he thought Australia was a Wonderland. I was their first Australian Girl. Like Marly, I grew up in the western suburbs of Melbourne, behind a carpet factory. Braybrook was a very multicultural neighbourhood and I had friends from all over the world.

My husband Nick is from countryside Corryong. We have travelled all over the world, but when we think of home we always think of Australia.

HOW I BECAME AN
AUSTRALIAN
GIRL

by *Lucia Masciullo*

I was born and grew up in Italy, a beautiful country to visit, but also a difficult country to live in for new generations.

In 2006, I packed up my suitcase and I left Italy with the man I love. We bet on Australia. I didn't know much about Australia before coming — I was just looking for new opportunities, I guess.

And I liked it right from the beginning! Australian people are resourceful, open-minded and always with a smile on their faces. I think all Australians keep in their blood a bit of the pioneer heritage, regardless of their own birthplace.

Here I began a new life and now I'm doing what I always dreamed of: I illustrate stories. Here is the place where I'd like to live and to grow up my children, in a country that doesn't fear the future.

*V*ietnam is a small country in Southeast Asia once owned by France and occupied by Japan during World War II. From 1955 to 1975, Vietnam was divided into the North and South and both were at war with each other. Communist North Vietnam wanted Vietnam to become one nation, but the South wanted to remain independent. American and Australian troops helped South Vietnam but ultimately lost the war.

After the war ended, thousands of South Vietnamese were sent to 're-education' camps. The Chinese in Vietnam, like Marly's family, were called the Hoa. The new government took away many of their businesses and taxed them heavily. Many Hoa fled Vietnam from 1978 onwards for a better life abroad.

From 1975 to 1995, almost 800,000 people left Vietnam by boat. The first destination for these 'boat people' were the neighbouring countries of Malaysia, Indonesia, Thailand, the Philippines, Singapore and Hong Kong. Many of the refugees did not survive the journey. Like Marly's cousins, boat people stayed in refugee camps in these countries until most were resettled in France, Canada, Australia, Germany and the United Kingdom.

Australia's 'White Australia Policy' discouraged non-white immigrants from settling here. But the White Australia Policy ended in 1973, and the refugees from Vietnam were the first large group of Asians to be resettled in Australia. They lived in working-class suburbs like Sunshine in Victoria and Cabramatta in NSW. A quarter of the refugees from Vietnam in Australia were Chinese, like Marly.

Vietnamese refugees often faced the journey in fishing boats like this one. The trip was treacherous and many people did not survive because of storms, pirates, and overcrowded and unsafe boats.

DID YOU KNOW THAT IN THE 1980s . . .

Uluru was handed back to its traditional Aboriginal owners in 1986.

The first-ever mobile phone (Fuji), compact discs (CDs) and laptop (IBM) were invented.

The Rubik's cube was invented in 1977 by Professor Erno Rubik and first known as the Hungarian Magic Cube. It was made available to the world as the Rubik's Cube in 1980 and became Toy of the Year that year.

Prince William was born in 1982, and becomes second in line to the British throne after his father Charles.

Michael Jackson released his album *Thriller* in 1982, the best-selling album of all time.

In 1982 computer scientist Scott Fahlman invented the use of the Smiley :-) as an emoticon!

In 1983 China's population reached one billion.

In 1984 'Advance Australia Fair' became Australia's national anthem, and green and gold became Australia's official national colours.

Want to find out more?

Turn the page for a sneak peek at Book 2

'I've got a job,' Marly bragged to her classmates at school on a Monday morning. 'A real job.'

'Oh yeah?' said Kane. 'What do you do then?' Kane was the class eavesdropper. He liked getting involved in other people's business.

'I iron collars.'

'What, doing housework for your mum? That's not a real job,' replied Kane.

'No, I mean ironing collars on shirts, Kane, you derbrain. The sorts of shirts you buy in the shops.'

'Isn't that illegal? You're still only ten.'

'No, it's not, because my mum is my boss,' said Marly. 'She's the one paying me.'

'Then that's not real work,' sneered

Kane. 'It's pocket money.'

'Not if you get paid ten cents a collar.'

'Then you're stupid. That's not even worth it.' Kane shrugged.

'Do the maths, you idiot. I can iron one hundred collars over the weekend easy.'

Kane thought for a while, then his eyebrows shot up. 'Woah,' he breathed. 'That's ten dollars. What are you going to do with that much money?'

Marly knew exactly what she was going to do. For the past month, all the kids at school had been collecting Garbage Gang swap cards. The Garbage Gang were cartoon characters that weren't on television, or comic strips, or anywhere else except on special Garbage Gang cards. They were modelled on Cabbage Patch Kids, with similar puffy faces and dimpled hands, but the Garbage Gang had names like Virus Iris, Potty Scotty and Dead Ted. Ray Decay was missing most of his teeth and surrounded by lollies, while Art Apart had his arms and legs loose on the floor. Nasty Nick looked like a vampire, and Guillo Tina was just about to get her head chopped off. There was also Flat Pat who was run over by a steamroller, and Bony Joanie who was a skeleton.

Even the boys collected these cards. 'Wouldn't it be cool if they really did make Garbage Gang dolls?' Marly had heard Kane say to Graham one day. 'I would totally get Adam Bomb.' Adam Bomb was a boy character in white socks and a blue suit, detonating the black box of a bomb to make his head explode.

Marly didn't have a single Garbage Gang card. Her parents would not allow them.

'What a waste of money,' her mother scoffed. Her mother would not let them buy anything that they could make, and cousin Rosie – who had recently changed her name from Tuyet – was great at making things. For her last birthday, Rosie had made Marly a set of UNO cards. Each one was cut in brown cardboard the exact size and shape of a UNO card, with the rounded corners. They had been covered with white paper and coloured in with texta. It must have taken Rosie hours to make the set. Marly loved playing with her cousin's cards at home when they came to visit, but she knew they weren't the real deal – they didn't have the same satisfying slipperiness as the genuine UNO, and they were too thick. It was not a present she could bring to school and share with her friends.

'Ask your cousin to make you the Rubbish Bin cards,' Marly's mother had suggested. 'She's a good drawer.'

'It's not the same, Mum!'

'Well, I'm not letting you waste a dollar on bits of cardboard. That's ridiculous. A dollar will get us three bunches of green leafy vegetables.'

Every afternoon, Marly would come home and have to wash these vegetables because her mother was busy working on her sewing machine. On weekends, her aunty Tam would come over to help her mother sew. That was when Marly got to see her two cousins, eleven-year-old Rosie and seven-year-old Jacky. They lived fifteen minutes away on the seventeenth floor of a brown-and-grey block of Housing Commission flats.

A week ago, Rosie had been in the garage ironing a stack of men's shirts very carefully when Marly called her out to play. 'I can't, Marly, I'm working,' she said.

'What do you mean you're working?' Marly stuck her head into the garage.

'She's helping us iron shirts,' said Marly's mum. 'Unlike you, always mucking about all the time. And she's earning money.'

Marly's ears perked up. 'What?'

'That's right. For every shirt she irons, she gets paid eighty cents.'

'Ten shirts, eight dollars,' replied Rosie

with a smile that Marly thought looked more like a smirk.

'I want to iron shirts too!' demanded Marly. 'How come you never let me do stuff like that?'

'Because you're too easily distracted, that's why,' scolded Marly's mum. 'And you do things half-heartedly before you decide you'd rather be playing outside with Jacky. Do you think we'd let you hold a hot iron to a shirt that your aunty and I have spent three hours making?'

'No fair!' protested Marly. She was so cross – she'd learned a lot since Rosie and Jacky had come to live with them, and her mother had often said how helpful she'd become around the house.

In the end, her aunty Tam suggested that they let her iron the interfacing onto the shirt collars that were stacked in a cardboard box on the floor. The interfacing was what made shirt collars stiff. It was a little piece of plastic material that you slipped inside the collar of the shirt and then ironed into place.

'Those are pretty easy to do,' said Aunty Tam.

But Marly's mum still hesitated. 'What if she burns one?'

'Well,' replied Aunty Tam, 'far better than sewing a whole new shirt. It's just a detached collar.'

'So how much do I get paid for each collar?' Marly asked.

'Aiyoh!' her mother cried. 'Consider yourself lucky we're giving you this experience! Will you listen to her — talking about making money already and not even grown up yet!'

Aunty Tam laughed. 'Come on, if we're going to pay Rosie, we'd better pay Marly as well. She's an enterprising girl.'

'Fine then,' sighed Marly's mother. 'Fine. We'll pay you ten cents a collar. And don't you dare complain! Your cousin's ironing is much more difficult than yours.

All you have to do is run a hot iron on this strip of interfacing so that it sticks to the inside of the shirt collar.'

And that was how Marly got her first weekend job.

'I'm going to get the whole set of Garbage Gang cards,' Marly had repeated to her classmates that Friday afternoon.

All week she had shown off about it, because she wanted to make sure at least some of the kids brought their own cards to school on Monday so she could swap with them.

Marly sat listlessly on the sofa on Monday morning, watching a television commercial before school.

'Come on Marly, get a move on!' Her mum unzipped her schoolbag and shoved in her sandwich and Prima juice.

Marly didn't move. She was still angry at her mother for tricking her.

Marly's mum stood in front of the television and switched it off. 'You might not care about being late but that doesn't mean you can make your brother late too.'

'I'm so tired from working all weekend,' Marly complained as her mother walked them to school. 'I ironed a hundred collars and didn't even get paid.'

'Of course you got paid,' said Marly's mother, losing her patience. 'You got paid very well.'

Marly heaved a big sigh and continued walking. It was drizzling and that made her even grumpier. Soon they reached the school gate. Marly could see a gang of kids already there, waiting for her.

She felt suddenly ill. How was she going to explain why she didn't have the cards?

Follow the story of your favourite
Australian girls and you will see that there
is a special charm on the cover of each book
that tells you something about the story.

Here they all are. You can tick them
off as you read each one.

Meet Grace

**A Friend
for Grace**

**Grace
and Glory**

**A Home
for Grace**

MEET LETTY

**LETTY AND THE
STRANGER'S
LACE**

**LETTY
ON THE LAND**

**LETTY'S
CHRISTMAS**

Meet Poppy

*Poppy at
Summerhill*

*Poppy and
the Thief*

*Poppy
Comes Home*

Meet Rose

Rose on Wheels

*Rose's
Challenge*

Rose in Bloom

Meet Nellie

**Nellie and
the Letter**

Nellie's Luck

**Nellie's
Greatest Wish**

Meet Alice

**Alice and the
Apple Blossom Fair**

**Alice at
Peppermint Grove**

**Peacetime
for Alice**

Meet Lina

*Lina's
Many Lives*

*Lina
at the Games*

*A Lesson
for Lina*

Meet Ruby

Ruby and the
Country Cousins

School Days
for Ruby

Ruby
of Kettle Farm

Meet Daisy

Daisy All Alone

**Daisy in the
Mansion**

**Daisy
on the Road**

Meet Pearlie

Pearlie's Pet Rescue

Pearlie the Spy

*Pearlie
Finds a Friend*

Meet Marly

Marly's Business

*Marly
and the Goat*

*Marly Walks
on the Moon*

3190106042136 1